Usborne
Aesop's Fables

Anna Milbourne
Illustrated by Linda Edwards

Designed by Amanda Gulliver
and Nelupa Hussain
Edited by Gillian Doherty

Contents

Usborne
Aesop's
Fables

The boy who cried wolf

"Nothing exciting ever happens to me," sighed the shepherd boy. "Looking after sheep is as dull as ditchwater." He herded his flock up a steep hillside to the lush, green meadow at the top and flung himself down on the grass. "I'm not cut out to be a shepherd," he thought, plucking the petals off a daisy. "I want more excitement, more drama. I wish I were a lion tamer – I'd make a magnificent lion tamer."

He grabbed his crook and jumped to his feet. "Back! Back!" he shouted commandingly, thrusting the stick at an imaginary lion. The sheep scattered in alarm. "Stupid sheep," snorted the boy. "There aren't any real lions around here!"

Feeling glum, he slumped back down onto the grass.

"But how on earth can I be a lion tamer if there aren't any lions," he said miserably.

"I suppose I'll just have to make do with these boring old sheep."

He glanced across at the thick, dark forest on the other side of the meadow. "There are supposed to be wolves, though," he murmured, his eyes lighting up at the thought. "The farmer's always telling me to keep a good look out for them... He'd go wild if I said I'd seen a wolf," he giggled mischievously. "What a drama that would be."

In the fields below, the farmer and his farmhands were hard at work weeding a crop of cabbages when they heard a shout. "Help! Wolf!"

"Quick," called the farmer. "The shepherd needs our help." He seized his spade and started running up the hill. The farmhands raced behind him. And behind them rushed the farmer's wife, the stable boy and the milkmaid, all determined to save the shepherd and his sheep from the wolf.

But they dashed bravely over the brow of the hill only to find the sheep grazing peacefully and the shepherd grinning from ear to ear. Utterly bewildered, the farmer stopped dead in his tracks, and the farmhands, the farmer's wife, the stable boy and the milkmaid all went crashing into one another behind him.

"Where's the wolf?" panted the farmer, brandishing his spade in a wolf-threatening way.

"There isn't one," laughed the boy. "I just wanted

to see whether you'd come."

"You mean we've run all the way up here for nothing?" spluttered the farmer.

"I wouldn't say for nothing," the boy said naughtily. "You've brightened up my day with your red faces." And he burst into a fit of giggles.

"What a waste of time," roared the furious farmer. He turned around and stomped off down the hillside, the grumbling farmhands, his wife, the stable boy and the milkmaid all following behind.

The next afternoon, there was another cry from the top of the hill. "WOLF! Help, a wolf!" Once again, the farmer and his farmhands flung down their tools and charged up the hillside. Behind them scrambled the farmer's wife, the stable boy and the milkmaid, all anxious to save the shepherd and his sheep.

But when they arrived at the top, they found the shepherd doubled up with laughter. "You should have seen yourselves scrambling up the hill," he gasped. "You looked so funny!"

Glowering with rage, the farmer and his farmhands, the farmer's wife, the stable boy and the milkmaid turned around. Without a single word, they all marched back down the hill.

"That's certainly cheered me up," chuckled the shepherd. "Those fools, thinking there was a real wolf!"

Suddenly, he heard a bone-chilling growl. He looked around and his heart almost stopped in fright. A huge wolf was slinking out of the forest. Its eyes were blood-red and its jaws hung open, showing two rows of terrible teeth. He stared, frozen to the spot, as the wolf crept towards his flock. Then, all at once, it pounced. With a flick of its jaws, the wolf devoured a startled sheep on the spot.

"WOLF!" screamed the shepherd at the top of his voice. The wolf pounced on a second sheep and gobbled it up. Then it ate a third, and a fourth. "HELP!" yelled the shepherd, backing away from the enormous creature.

Down in the cabbage field, the farmer was shaking his head. "That boy is up to his tricks again," he said to the farmhands. "Just ignore him."

In the farmhouse kitchen, the farmer's wife tutted and said to the milkmaid. "That boy's trying to play a joke on us again. Pay no attention."

"You're not going to fool me this time, you rascal," muttered the stable boy as he swept the stable.

"Somebody help!" wailed the shepherd. But nobody came. The boy watched helplessly as the wolf slaughtered his flock, one by one. When the last sheep was gone, the wolf turned to face the shepherd, licking its lips greedily.

"You're not eating me!" squealed the terrified boy, and he bolted down the hillside as fast as his legs would carry him. The wolf, now almost as round as a barrel, staggered back into the dark forest.

"There was a wolf!" gasped the shepherd as he burst through the gates of the farm. "Why didn't you come?"

Seeing the boy's tear-stained face and knocking knees, the farmer realized that this time the shepherd really had been telling the truth. "What did you expect?" he said to the trembling boy. "I'm afraid you cried 'Wolf' once too often."

The busy ant and the singing grasshopper

"Why don't you stop and enjoy the sun?" the grasshopper called to the ant as she hurried past.

The ant put down the large seed she was carrying and sighed. "I have too much to do," she said. "If I don't gather food for our store, my family won't have anything to eat in the winter."

"Who cares about winter?" replied the grasshopper drowsily. "You should enjoy the summer while it lasts." Closing his eyes, he began to sing a lazy summer song. He sang of the butterflies fluttering by; he sang of the flowers' sweet perfume; and he sang of long, summer days that seemed as though they would last forever.

The next day, the day after, and the one after that, the ant worked hard while the grasshopper did nothing but sunbathe and sing. Every time the ant passed by, the grasshopper invited her to stop for a while. But every time, the ant answered, "I can't stop now. I'm far too busy."

One day, when the summer was nearly over, the grasshopper said to the ant, "You must have enough in your store by now. You've been slaving away all summer."

"Have you any idea how big my family is?" the ant replied briskly. "Besides, don't you think you ought to be putting something away for yourself? I've heard it's going to be a cold winter. You'll need more than a song to keep you warm." And with that, she hurried on her way.

The grasshopper paid no attention. "Who wants to waste their life making preparations?" he said carelessly, and settled down under a dandelion to sing himself to sleep.

But, as the days went by, the sun began to lose its warmth. The butterflies disappeared and the leaves on the trees turned red and gold. Still, the grasshopper did nothing but sing. A chill crept in from the north, making him shiver. Men came to harvest their crops and before long the grasshopper found himself alone in an empty field, listening to the wind whistle through the stubbly stalks and howl across the sky.

He was cold and hungry, and he didn't feel much like singing any more. Thinking of all the food the ant had put away, the grasshopper decided to ask her for help.

He hopped along the ant's well-worn path and found her little doorway in the soil. "Little ant! Little ant!" he called. "Are you at home?"

The ant scurried to answer the door. All her tiny daughters and sons and nieces and nephews came too. They crowded into the doorway, curious to see who their visitor was.

"My! You really do have a big family!" exclaimed the grasshopper. "I was wondering," he continued hopefully, "whether you could spare me a morsel from your store. I'm cold and hungry now that winter has arrived."

"But what happened to your own store?" asked one of the tiny ants.

"Was it washed away in a terrible flood?" shrilled another.

"Or stolen by a big, scary bird?" suggested a third.

"Not exactly," said the grasshopper awkwardly. "I mean to say — I didn't actually make a store."

"But what were you doing all summer?" asked the tiniest ant of all.

The grasshopper blushed. "Not much," he said. "In fact..." he mumbled, looking down at his feet, "I wasn't really doing anything at all."

All of the tiny ants gasped in shock.

The mother ant frowned. "So now you expect to come and live off my store, do you? I worked hard all summer long to make my store, grasshopper," she said firmly, "and I have over a thousand mouths to feed."

"Oh dear," sighed the grasshopper. "Perhaps I should have prepared for the future a little after all, instead of just sunbathing and singing all summer." He turned to leave.

"Wait a moment," a tiny ant piped up. "Did you say you could sing?"

The grasshopper looked back and nodded. "That's right," he said. "That's one thing I *can* do."

"Oh, sing us a song!" cried the tiny ant.

"Perhaps he can sing for his supper," suggested another. "Can he, Mama? Can he?"

"Please let him," begged all the other tiny ants.

The mother ant folded her arms and looked sternly at the grasshopper. "Very well," she said. "But just this once."

And so all the ants settled down to listen to the grasshopper sing. It was a beautiful and haunting song. He sang of sunny days and butterflies; he sang of falling leaves and the howling wind; and he sang of the wisdom of ants, who work all summer long so they have something to put in their bellies when the cold winter sets in.

King of the birds

There was a twittering and a fluttering down by the river. Since dawn, the birds had been busy preening their feathers and polishing their beaks in preparation for the big day ahead. The mighty god Zeus was coming to see them. After watching all the birds in a grand parade, he was going to name one of them king.

"Just think," said the bird of paradise, gazing smugly at his own reflection in the water. "In a few hours, the prettiest bird will be king."

"Or perhaps the most elegant," said the swan.

"Or the most royal-looking," said the hoopoe bird, raising his orange crest like a crown.

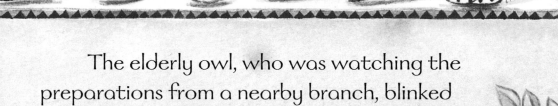

The elderly owl, who was watching the preparations from a nearby branch, blinked thoughtfully. "Perhaps Zeus will choose the cleverest bird to be king," he suggested.

All the other birds fell about laughing. None of them cared two hoots for cleverness.

"It's obvious," said the peacock, spreading out his glorious tail so that it hid the bird of paradise from view. "The most beautiful bird will win."

The jackdaw looked down at his dull, black plumage and gave a miserable sigh. If Zeus was going to choose the most beautiful bird to be king, then he didn't stand a chance.

Glumly, he watched the parrot preening his wonderful blue and yellow tail. A single, sunshine-yellow feather floated past him and settled on the ground. By now, hundreds of feathers from the preening birds were scattered all over the riverbank. "So many lovely, wasted feathers," he said sadly. "If only I had plumes like those..."

Then he had an idea. Hopping along the ground, he began to collect the unwanted feathers. None of the birds noticed the plain old jackdaw as he hopped about among them. He stuffed as many feathers as he could possibly carry into his beak and flew off into the forest.

By noon, everyone was ready for the parade – apart from the hens, who were in a last-minute flap. All the birds gathered at the edge of the forest to wait for Zeus.

The bowerbirds had
arranged flowers and
shells around a rocky throne
where the god was to sit. They were just
adding the finishing touches when there was
a loud clap of thunder and Zeus appeared.

The nightingales sang a song of welcome
and the penguins ushered the god to his seat.
The bird of paradise brought him sweet nectar
to drink and a team of hummingbirds kept him
cool by fanning their wings.

"Let the parade begin!" boomed Zeus.
The birds scurried and fluttered into a long line
that stretched all the way back into the forest.

Then, one by one, they began to strut, stalk, waddle and hop past Zeus, each bird hoping to dazzle the god with his finery so that he would be made king.

Zeus watched carefully. First came the majestic golden eagle, followed by a pair of elegant, snow-white storks. A group of penguins marched by in dinner jackets, and the kingfisher darted through the air, his chest thrust out to show off his lovely orange waistcoat. There were proud roosters and scarlet ibises, jewel-like hummingbirds and flamboyant flamingoes. Each bird, from the flounciest peacock to the sleekest swan, appeared even more beautiful than the last. The line of birds seemed to go on forever, but Zeus gave every one of them his undivided attention, until the afternoon sun faded and dropped behind the trees.

When the last little bird in the parade had hopped past, Zeus cleared his throat ready to speak. Suddenly, there was a rustling in the forest. Everyone's eyes turned to the trees. There was a pause – then out of the forest stepped a strange and exotic-looking bird. None of the others had ever seen it before.

The bird had a dazzling array of feathers – golden ones and scarlet ones, sugar-pink ones and emerald-green ones, speckled ones and striped ones – and an exquisite fan-like tail that shimmered with turquoise spots. To top it all, he wore a crown of luxurious, ruby-red feathers on his head.

All the other birds stared in dismay as the beautiful stranger strutted towards Zeus. It seemed to be enjoying the attention hugely. When it reached the front of the crowd, it turned around very slowly, to show itself off from every side. Then it bowed gracefully to Zeus, bending so low that its crown touched the ground in front of the god's feet.

"Well I never," said Zeus in astonishment. "Until this moment, I wasn't sure who to name as king. All the birds I have seen today were equally beautiful, each in its own way. But now it seems the choice is clear. This bird has a little bit of everything..."

The strange bird nodded excitedly and all the others groaned with disappointment.

"Hold on a minute," said the peacock, staring very hard at the new bird's tail feathers. "Did you say a little bit of *everything*? I think you might be right." He pushed through the other birds to get a closer look. "That's MINE!" he screeched, snatching a long, turquoise-spotted feather from the stranger's tail.

"And those are mine!" shouted the flamingo. He stretched his long neck over the penguins and plucked a row of sugar-pink feathers from the stranger's back.

The crowd of birds pressed in closely around the poor stranger. "You've got some of my head feathers," whooped the hoopoe accusingly.

"And my wing feathers!" squawked the parrot. One after the other, the birds began to snatch back their feathers and, little by little, the strange, fantastic-looking bird lost all its bright plumage. Soon, it didn't look very strange or fantastic at all. It looked very ordinary and really rather crestfallen.

"It's the jackdaw!" hissed the swan in disgust.

"So it is," said a stork, looking down his beak at the unhappy bird. "What a cheat!"

"I can't believe Zeus nearly made a jackdaw king instead of ME," screeched the peacock.

"It would have been even worse if he had chosen you, you vain creature!" scoffed the flamingo.

"You can talk, you pink-plumed dandy!" yelled the ornamental duck.

Squawking and screeching, clawing and flapping, the birds set upon one another in a rage. Feathers flew everywhere as they pecked and plucked. Before long, not a single one of them looked in the least like a king. The rooster's comb was reduced to tatters, the vulture's neck had been pecked bare and the parrot had squawked itself blue in the face.

Zeus sat and watched them for a few moments. Then he stood up, looking utterly disgusted. "What a bunch of featherbrains," he muttered, and vanished in a clap of thunder.

Startled by the noise, the birds stopped bickering and looked around. They'd forgotten all about Zeus. "But – but – but," stuttered the woodpecker, "he hasn't made any of us king."

"Come back!" cried the rooster.

But the only reply was a disapproving rumble from the sky, as a few black rainclouds gathered on the horizon.

The jackdaw struggled out from the flock of dishevelled birds and flew over to sit by the owl, who was nodding off in a tree. "I suppose that wasn't such a bright idea, was it?" he said humbly.

"Probably not," agreed the sleepy owl. "I find it's always easier just to be oneself. There's nobody else who does it better, after all."

The donkey
and the wolf

A plump donkey was munching happily through a patch
of clover one afternoon when a low, dangerous snarl nearly
made her jump out of her skin. She swung around and saw
a vicious-looking wolf running across the field in her direction.
His eyes were narrowed and his teeth were bared. He looked
very, very hungry.

"It's too late to run," thought the donkey in a panic. "I'm
done for!" By now, the wolf was so close that she could see the
glints in his eyes and the saliva dripping from his teeth. She
racked her brains desperately for a way to escape.

When the wolf was a mere whisker away, the donkey let
out a yell. "Ouch! My poor hoof," she brayed. "How that
thorn hurts!"

"I wouldn't worry about a little thing like that," said the
wolf, licking his lips. "It won't bother you for much longer."

The donkey sighed. "If you're planning to eat me," she said,
"you may as well get on with it. But you should probably take
the thorn out of my hoof before you start. Otherwise it'll stick
in your throat on the way down."

"That's very thoughtful of you," leered the wolf. "I do like
a helpful lunch." He bent down to examine the donkey's hoof.

"Where's this thorn then?" he said. "Let me have a look."

The donkey lifted one back hoof a little way off the ground. "It's in this foot," she said. "Can you see it?"

"No…" said the wolf, and bent a little closer.

"It's right in the middle," replied the donkey, lifting her foot a little higher. "Can you see it now?"

The wolf bent even closer, so that his nose was almost touching the donkey's hoof. "No…" he said.

"Really?" said the donkey. "Perhaps that's because there isn't one!" Then she kicked the wolf as hard as she could with both of her back feet. He flew head over heels and landed with a yelp halfway across the field.

The donkey watched gleefully as the dazed wolf picked himself up and slunk away into the forest. "Hee hee, haw haw," she laughed. "I do like a helpful wolf!"

How the tortoise got his shell

"We're going to a party!" shouted the monkey excitedly, clutching a gold-stamped invitation in her paw. "Zeus, the great thunder god, is getting married tomorrow and we're all invited."

Throughout the morning, the skies had been filled with bluebirds, swallows and swifts dropping invitations outside every animal's home. In all the forests and meadows, seas and skies, creatures were squeaking, hopping, singing and chattering with sheer delight.

"Gods throw the very best parties," said the monkey enthusiastically. "Everyone's going to be there."

"Not me," said the tortoise, popping his sleepy head out of his doorway to see what all the fuss was about. "I don't think I can be bothered."

"You can't be bothered?"
exclaimed the monkey in surprise.

"No," yawned the tortoise. "I think
I'd rather just stay at home." He crawled out
of his doorway to lie in the sun. In those days,
the tortoise didn't have a shell. He was just a bare,
wrinkly animal, who never strayed far from his comfortable
burrow in the ground.

"Well," said the monkey, "you'll be the only one!"

And she was right. The next day, animals from all four
corners of the world trotted and scampered, scurried and flew
to Zeus' summer palace for the party.

And what a party it was! Garlands of flowers and bright
banners hung between the trees, beautiful fountains showered
glittering droplets, and heavenly music wove its way through
the air like gold and silver threads.

Zeus and his bride showed the guests to their places. Laid
out on long tables beneath the trees was the most wonderful
feast, with dish after dish of food to suit each and every
animal. There were carrot cakes for the rabbit and seed rolls for
the birds, honey buns for the bear and all the banana splits the
monkey could eat.

As everyone sat down to the feast, Zeus suddenly noticed that there was an empty place. "Who's missing?" he asked the squirrel.

"The tortoise," said the squirrel, munching her way joyfully through a large nut cluster.

"Where is he?" asked Zeus.

The squirrel shrugged. "He didn't come," she said. "I'm not sure why. Nobody else would have missed this for the world!"

Zeus nodded, looking thoughtful.

After everyone had eaten their fill, the band started to play. Zeus got up with his wife and danced a merry jig and, one by one, the animals left their tables and joined in. They danced in circles and they danced in lines, holding hands together or whirling each other around in pairs. Night fell and the moon appeared, shining like a huge lantern in the sky. On and on they danced, all through the night. Soon, the moon slipped away and the waking sun began to stroke her fingers across the sky.

As his tired, happy guests prepared to go home, Zeus gave each of them a gift. He gave a song to the nightingale and a hop to the hare, stripes to the zebra and a pair of humps to the camel. Home the guests went, delighted with their gifts, their ears still ringing with the sound of the music.

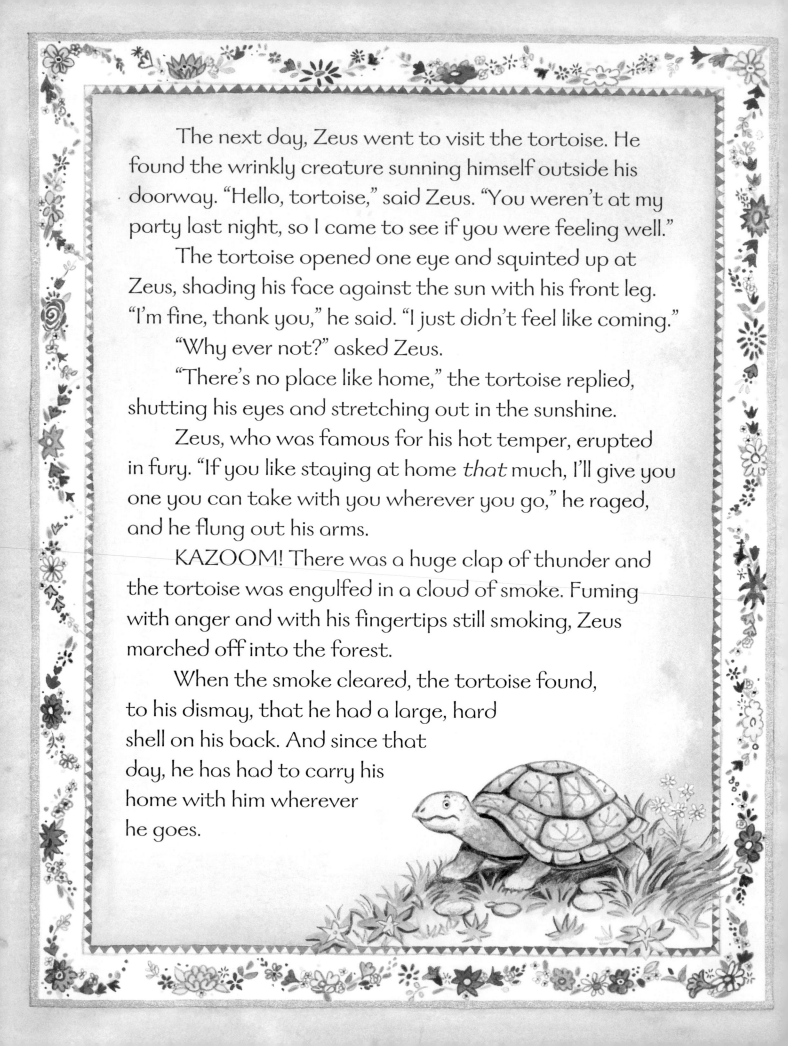

The next day, Zeus went to visit the tortoise. He found the wrinkly creature sunning himself outside his doorway. "Hello, tortoise," said Zeus. "You weren't at my party last night, so I came to see if you were feeling well."

The tortoise opened one eye and squinted up at Zeus, shading his face against the sun with his front leg. "I'm fine, thank you," he said. "I just didn't feel like coming."

"Why ever not?" asked Zeus.

"There's no place like home," the tortoise replied, shutting his eyes and stretching out in the sunshine.

Zeus, who was famous for his hot temper, erupted in fury. "If you like staying at home *that* much, I'll give you one you can take with you wherever you go," he raged, and he flung out his arms.

KAZOOM! There was a huge clap of thunder and the tortoise was engulfed in a cloud of smoke. Fuming with anger and with his fingertips still smoking, Zeus marched off into the forest.

When the smoke cleared, the tortoise found, to his dismay, that he had a large, hard shell on his back. And since that day, he has had to carry his home with him wherever he goes.

The clever fox and the vain crow

A hungry crow was flying over a village one morning when he spotted a tray of freshly baked pies cooling on a window ledge. "What luck," he thought, and swooped down to steal one for his breakfast.

Clutching the steaming pie in his beak, he flew into a nearby garden and landed on the branch of an apple tree. He was just about to gobble up his fine breakfast when a fox came nosing along beneath the tree.

Catching a waft of the delicious-smelling pie, the fox stopped and looked up. When he spotted the crow, a crafty smile crept across his face.

"That fox wants a piece of my pie," thought the crow. "Well, he can't have any, no matter how much he begs."

But, to the crow's surprise, the fox didn't even ask for a piece of the pie. Instead, he stepped back a little, cocked his head to one side and said, "My! What a beautiful bird you are."

The crow was very pleased. He'd always thought he was wonderfully good-looking, and so he wasn't in the least bit surprised that a passing fox should be struck by his beauty.

31

He looked up and down the branch for a safe place to put down his pie while he thanked the fox, but he couldn't see one. So he kept hold of it and gave a little bow instead, to show his appreciation.

"What extraordinarily glossy feathers you have," said the fox admiringly.

The crow puffed out his chest.

"And a fine, broad chest," added the fox.

The crow strutted clumsily back and forth, practically falling off the branch with pride.

"And the way you move," gasped the fox. "You're the most graceful creature I've ever seen."

The compliments went straight to the crow's head, and he did a twirl to show off his tail feathers.

"I heard that Zeus was trying to choose a king of the birds not so long ago," said the fox. "Is that true?"

The crow, with the pie still wedged firmly in his beak, nodded vigorously.

"Why didn't he choose you?" exclaimed the fox. "A fine fellow like you would make a fabulous king."

The bird shrugged, and his mind filled with visions of himself sitting on a throne, wearing a jewel-encrusted crown and being waited on wing and foot by all the other birds. He was really very taken with the idea. In fact, now that the fox mentioned it, he couldn't understand why Zeus *hadn't* made him king of the birds.

"I suppose
the one thing
you're lacking,"
said the fox, "is a
voice." He looked
up at the crow slyly.
"A bird without a voice
wouldn't make a very
good king."

"I HAVE got a voice,"
squawked the crow. But, of course, as he
opened his beak, the precious pie tumbled to
the ground. Before the crow had even finished
his sentence, the fox had pounced on the pie and
gobbled it all up.

"It's a pity you don't have a brain as well,"
laughed the fox, licking the crumbs off his paws.
"Then you'd have made a perfect king!"

The sun and the north wind

"I'm much stronger than you," the north wind boasted to the sun. "I can blow ships across the sea and birds right out of the sky. I can push trees over and tear whole roofs off houses. What can you do?"

"Ripping things to shreds isn't my style," replied the gentle sun. "I coax flowers into bloom and help the trees to grow."

"Pah! That's child's play," scoffed the wind. "In a test of strength, I'd beat you any day."

Just then, he spotted a man walking along below them. "I know," he said to the sun. "Let's have a competition. Whoever can remove that man's coat wins."

"All right," agreed the sun.

"I'll go first, so you can see how it's done," blustered the wind, and he blew a few playful gusts to knock the man's hat off.

But the man seized his hat just in time and rammed it firmly back onto his head.

The north wind puffed out his cheeks and blew a little harder, making the man's coat flap open. He turned to the sun with a smug grin on his face. But, when he looked back again, the man had pulled his coat closed and buttoned it all the way up.

Frowning, the wind took a deep breath. Then he pursed his lips and blew with all his might.

The man staggered a little against the force of the wind's breath. His coat billowed out behind him, but it didn't come off.

The man wrestled a long scarf out of his bag and wrapped it tightly around his neck.

The north wind tugged impatiently at the man's coat, but the man just turned up his collar and stuffed his hands into his pockets. So the wind huffed and puffed. But the harder he blew, the more determined the man was to keep his coat on.

Eventually, the wind gave up. "That man is never going to give up his coat," he said. "He's just plain stubborn." And he moved aside to let the sun try.

The sun gazed at the man thoughtfully. He was hurrying along, his face pinched and his shoulders hunched against the cold. She began by sending down a few gentle, warming rays. The man relaxed his shoulders and looked relieved. He closed his eyes and tilted his face up to the sky.

The sun smiled encouragingly, bringing the whole landscape to life in her golden light. Birds started to sing and the flowers opened their petals. Slowly, the man unwound his scarf and undid his collar. The sun beamed happily.

"Humph!" said the wind. "Beginner's luck!"

With a warm chuckle, the sun shone even more brilliantly.

The man turned pink in the heat. He took off his hat and unbuttoned his coat.

"That's all very well," the wind said grumpily, "but you still need to get his coat off."

"All in good time," said the sun, and she shone and shone as brightly as she could.

The man stopped to wipe his brow. "What odd weather," he muttered, shaking his head in confusion. Then, to the wind's utter dismay, he took off his coat. Not only that, but he unbuttoned his shirt as well.

"All right, all right," sighed the north wind. "You win."

Down below, the man had reached the side of a lake. Suddenly, he kicked off his shoes and socks, stripped down to his underwear and dived into the water to cool down. The sun gave the north wind a radiant smile.

"There's no need to show off," snapped the wind in a huff, and blew away across the sky.

The dancing camel

It was midsummer's eve, and animals from all around the world were making their way to the top of a big, green hill for the midsummer party. Everyone was going – from the tiniest beetle to the most enormous elephant, the scaliest lizard to the furriest bear. The air hummed with excitement as they crawled, trotted, hopped and scurried up the hill.

"Let the party begin," roared the lion as the last few animals arrived at the top. The band struck up a tune at once. The kangaroo drummed on the ground with her feet, the elephant blew his trumpet, the goose honked, the cricket played his fiddle and the squirrel tooted away on a little wooden pipe.

Everyone chattered away cheerfully, catching up on each other's news. Everyone, that is, apart from the camel. The camel was a grumpy old soul. He grumbled away to whoever would listen. "This had better be a good party," he said. "I've come a very long way."

"You're not the only one," said the penguin. "Cheer up, camel. It'll be great — it always is."

The party got off to a wonderful start with all the usual games. The crocodile and the alligator played snap while the others had a game of leapfrog. After pin the tail on the donkey and piggy in the middle, all the animals joined in for hide-and-seek. The chameleon won, of course, as she did every year.

After the games, it was the tradition for each of the animals to entertain the others. This year was more fun than ever before. The dolphin put on a stunning water display, a pair of eagles performed a death-defying airshow and the orangutan did some spectacular acrobatics in the treetops.

Even the grumpy camel joined in, with a little persuasion from the mother kangaroo. He gave all the baby animals rides around the hill on his humps and told thrilling tales of his desert adventures. "Only once a year," he snorted. "Once a year only." But his eyes twinkled with amusement beneath his frown.

The funniest performance by far was the monkey's dance. The band struck up a lively tune and all the animals gathered around to watch. The monkey swung through the treetops in time to the beat, jitterbugged with a family of bats, danced cheek to cheek with a laughing baboon and then tangoed across the grass with a pretty lady skunk. The audience was utterly captivated. They clapped in time to the music and giggled and gasped at the monkey's daring dance moves.

For his grand finale, the monkey sprang high into the air, turned a triple somersault, and landed gracefully on the tip of the elephant's trunk.

All the animals cheered, clapped and hollered for more. Apart from one. "Harrumph!" snorted the camel. "I don't know why you're all clapping so hard. Anyone can dance like that."

"Don't be such an old grumpy humps," chided the mother kangaroo. "The monkey was doing what he's good at, and we should all cheer him for it. You should be happy doing what you're good at, rather than envying him. Camels can't dance."

"Of course they can," grunted the camel.

"Oh please," came a little voice, and the baby kangaroo poked his head out of his mother's pouch. "Won't you show us?"

Somewhat disgruntled, the camel loped slowly into the middle of the circle of animals and started to dance. He swayed his hips and knocked his knees together; he twitched his ears and nodded his head. The band played along as best they could, but it was really the most peculiar dance they'd ever seen and it was impossible for them to keep time. The camel gave a funny sideways hop and waggled his humps from side to side, but this made him lose his balance, and he staggered across the grass and crashed into the musicians.

"Watch where you're putting your feet," scolded the squirrel, picking up his trampled pipe. But the camel hardly noticed. Even when the band stopped playing in protest, he kept on dancing. He kicked out his legs and hit a tree, bringing a family of bluebirds tumbling down. He swung his tail and knocked a row of rabbits flying, and then he backed into the giraffe and trod on the elephant's toes.

41

"Stop!" shouted the kangaroo. "For goodness sake, stop!"

But the camel didn't stop. "I'm the best dancer," he panted. "See?" and he kept on flinging his clumsy feet all over the place. Soon, the animals were scrambling in all directions to get away from him.

It was only when the camel stomped on the lion's tail and was almost deafened by his ROAR of pain that he finally stopped. Looking around, he realized that his dance hadn't gone too well. The lion was glaring at him furiously, the mother kangaroo was shaking her head and the bushbaby was bawling her eyes out.

"Why isn't anyone clapping?" the camel asked crossly. "Didn't you like my dance?"

"Certainly not!" sniffed the llama.

"We liked you much better when you were giving us rides around the field," wailed the bushbaby.

"Or telling us stories of your desert adventures," added the bear cub.

"Oh," said the camel. He looked around at the broken musical instruments and the upset faces of all the animals. "I suppose it wasn't as much fun as the monkey's dance then?" he asked.

All the animals shook their heads in unison.

The camel looked up at the monkey, who was dangling from a branch above his head. "You do dance extraordinarily well," he said awkwardly.

The monkey clambered down the tree and gave the camel a friendly pat on the humps. "And you, my friend, can walk for miles and miles without water, can tell a gripping desert tale or two, and seem to be extremely popular for giving rides on your humps," he said.

"Yes, dear," said the kangaroo in her motherly way. "Everyone's good at something different. Aren't they?"

The camel looked down at the tear-stained bushbaby. "Well there's no need to cry," he said gruffly. "If it would cheer you up, I suppose I could give you another ride."

"Yes, please!" beamed the bushbaby.

The camel lowered his long eyelashes with pride and pleasure. "Hop on then," he said.

The hare and the tortoise

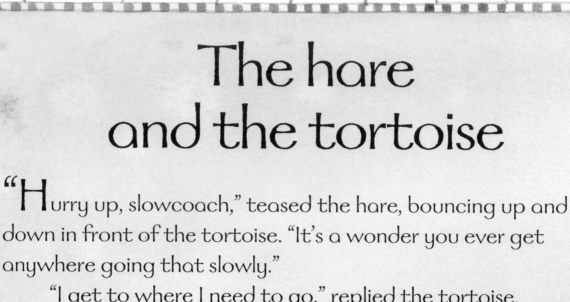

"Hurry up, slowcoach," teased the hare, bouncing up and down in front of the tortoise. "It's a wonder you ever get anywhere going that slowly."

"I get to where I need to go," replied the tortoise.

"And where's that?" mocked the hare. "About two inches away from where you started?"

"You leave him be," interrupted a small garden snail. "He's plenty fast enough."

"Maybe if you're used to going at a snail's pace," giggled the hare. "But if the tortoise and I had a race, you know very well who would win."

"You never know until you try," said the tortoise, with a wrinkly smile.

The hare missed a hop in amazement. "You can't seriously believe you'd be in with a chance?" he said, and even the snail looked a little surprised.

"I don't see why not," answered the tortoise solemnly.

"In that case," said the hare, "let's have a race. Tomorrow morning, at ten o'clock sharp, I'll race you from the top of the meadow to the barn at the bottom of the farmer's field."

"You're on," replied the tortoise.

"Goodness me," said the snail. "I have to see this," and she set out immediately, so as not to miss the finish.

Word about the race spread like wildfire. The snail told a fieldmouse, who whispered the news to a squirrel, who passed it on to a fox. A passing skylark overheard them and sang about it to anyone who would listen. By morning, animals from far and wide had come to watch the race.

At five to ten, the hare and the tortoise were limbering up on the starting line, as the crowds lined up along the racetrack. The hare did twenty star-jumps and a dozen high springs to warm up. The tortoise simply stretched out his wrinkly legs, one by one, and stared intently at the track before him.

"On your marks, please," called the pheasant, who had agreed to start the race. The hare and the tortoise crouched down, and a hush fell on the crowd. "Get set," said the pheasant. The onlookers craned forward. "GO!" shrieked the pheasant.

45

The hare shot off the starting line, bounding along at great speed. Within seconds, he was out of sight, zooming away in a cloud of dust. As the dust settled, the tortoise began to walk – very, *very* slowly – down the racetrack.

The crowd cheered and yelled encouragement at the tortoise. He was walking so slowly that many of them had shouted themselves hoarse by the time he actually passed them. But he kept on going at the same slow, steady pace.

Far ahead, the hare was speeding along, his long ears streaming out like banners behind him. Glancing over his shoulder, he realized that he'd left the tortoise a long way behind.

The hare was so confident of winning the race that he slowed down to wave at the clapping frogs and hollering foxes. He blew kisses to some leopard cubs and baby bears, and he even stopped to chat with a polar bear who had come all the way from the North Pole to see the race.

But soon, the hare had left the crowd a long way behind too. As the cheers died away, he could hear the humming of the bees and the twittering of the birds in the trees. It was a lovely, sunny day and, as he ran on up a hill, the hare began to feel a little sleepy. "I've got plenty of time," he thought. "I think I'll stop here for a little rest."

The hare hopped over to a tree beside the track and lay down in the dappled shade of its branches. "I'll just close my eyes," he murmured. "In a moment or two, I'll be as fresh as a daisy..." But in no time at all, the hare was fast asleep.

Meanwhile, the tortoise was still crawling along at the same slow pace. His supporters had started walking along the track beside him, taking turns to shout words of encouragement. The tortoise was going so slowly, however, that their enthusiasm began to wane. They exchanged doubtful glances over the tortoise's back, and, after a while, a fox said what they had all been thinking – "The hare must have reached the finishing line by now." But the tortoise paid no attention. With grim determination, he plodded on.

Slowly but surely, the tortoise climbed the hill and began to make his way past the tree. "I don't believe it," smirked the fox when he noticed the hare snoozing peacefully in the shade. "You may just be in with a chance, tortoise, old fellow." The tortoise's supporters let out a resounding cheer as he struggled over the top of the hill and down the other side.

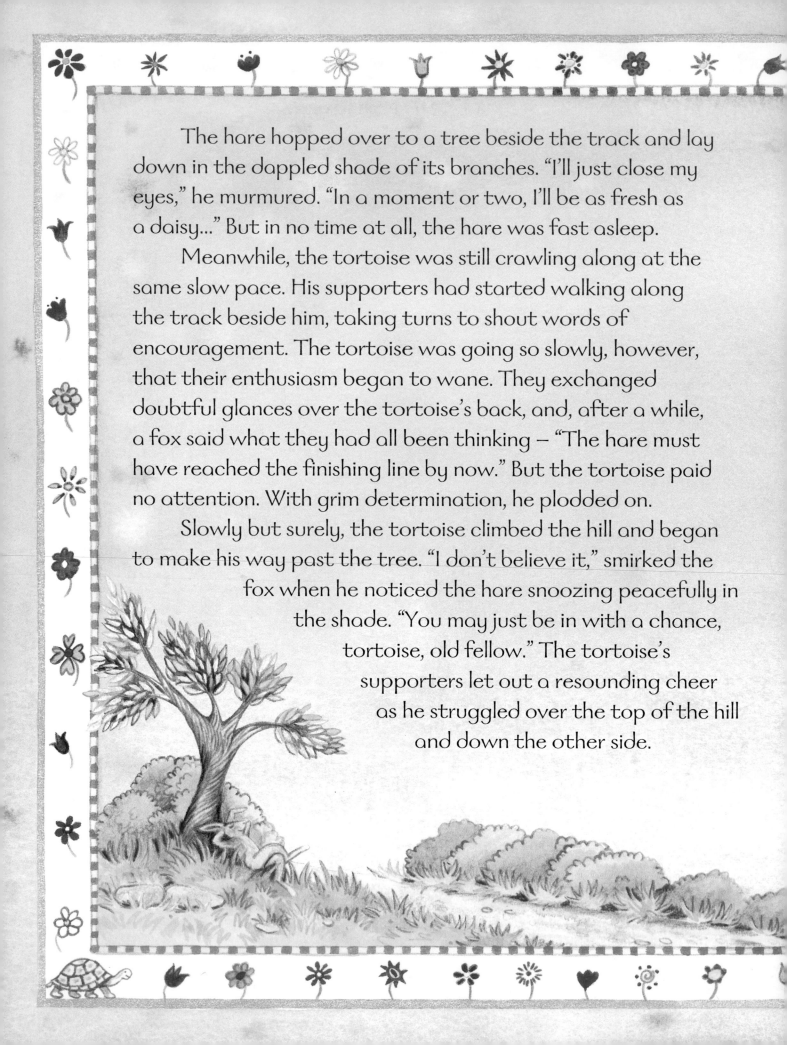

The cheers crept into the hare's slumber and he dreamed they were the roar of the crowd as he crossed the finishing line. His whiskers twitched with pride as he accepted an enormous golden trophy from a cheetah, who declared him to be the fastest runner in all the world.

By now, the tortoise had the finishing line in his sights. He kept plodding steadily along, without looking back over his shoulder or even glancing at his supporters, who, by now, were going wild with excitement. The little snail could hardly contain herself. "Come on, tortoise," she yelled, bobbing up and down on the finishing line. "You can do it!"

As the tortoise drew closer to the finishing line, the roar of the crowd got louder and louder, and the sleeping hare's ears pricked up a little as he slept. In his dream, the golden trophy had disappeared into thin air and the cheetah was roaring at him to hurry up.

Suddenly the hare woke up with a jolt. "Where's my trophy?" he muttered, squinting in the bright sunshine. And then he realized. "Oh no!" he gasped. "I haven't crossed the finishing line yet!"

He scrambled to his feet. Peering down the track, he could just see the tortoise nearing the line. "No!" he wailed, haring down the hill. In his panic, he ran faster than he'd ever run in his life.

"Good heavens," remarked the fox in an amused voice. "Whatever is that?"

All the animals stared in astonishment. Racing towards them, barely visible in a blur of speed, was the hare. He was gaining on the tortoise at the most amazing rate. The crowd held their breath as he shot down the track like a rocket.

"Hurry up, tortoise," screamed the little snail. "Hurry UP!" But the tortoise kept on walking at the same, agonizingly slow pace.

"I can't let a tortoise beat me," thought the hare. "I have to win," and he put on a frantic burst of speed. As he approached the finishing line, all he could hear was his blood thumping in his ears. Only a few more paces and victory would be his. But the tortoise was just raising his foot to take the winning step. In desperation, the hare threw himself at the finishing line.

But it was too late. The tortoise, going so slowly he could have been in slow-motion, stepped through the rope. A great roar broke out, and the crowd hoisted him onto their backs amid thunderous applause. The tortoise's face creased into a wide, triumphant smile.

The hare, meanwhile, sailed through the air and landed in the dust with a thud. "I'll never live this down," he groaned, covering his face with his paws.

"You see?" piped a small voice. It was the garden snail, looking so proud she was almost ready to pop. "Slow and steady wins the race!" .

The town mouse and the country mouse

"Lunch in the countryside – how divine!" exclaimed the town mouse. An invitation from his cousin had arrived by bird-post just moments before. "Fresh air, sunshine, peace and quiet..." the little mouse continued dreamily, as he stared out of the window at the busy street below. "I bet food tastes delicious when you're lazing in a meadow under the open sky."

"Excuse me," said the post-bird, who was waiting impatiently on the window ledge. "Will there be a reply?"

"Oh, yes, of course," said the mouse. "Please tell him I'd be delighted to come. I'll be there by noon tomorrow." The post-bird nodded and swooped away into the sky.

Early the next morning, the little mouse slipped under the door of the town house where he lived, and set off to visit his cousin in the countryside.

He scurried along the busy streets, dodging through hurrying feet and dashing through the roaring traffic, until he reached the train station. Hundreds of passengers were piling off a train onto the platform, clutching briefcases and umbrellas. The little mouse slipped nimbly through their legs and hopped onto the train just in time. The doors closed behind him and the train pulled out of the station.

Clambering onto an empty window seat, the town mouse watched as the busy town flew by. Houses and shops, alleys and streets, people and lampposts, buses and cars whizzed past. Gradually, they gave way to rolling green hills and wide, flowery meadows.

When the train eventually stopped at a sleepy country station, the mouse hopped off. He skipped down the station steps and found himself in a quiet country lane. The air hummed gently with bees, and the sky burned bright, silent blue. There wasn't a rushing crowd or a roaring bus anywhere to be seen.

The little mouse pulled the invitation out of his bag to look at the directions his cousin had sent him. "Take the lane downhill from the station. Then turn left into the field," he read, "and keep going until you can hear the river. Turn right after the third daisy and you'll find my door underneath the poppies."

In no time at all, the town mouse was knocking on his cousin's little wooden door under the shade of the nodding poppies. His cousin flung open the door, squeaking with delight. "How lovely to see you!" he cried. "Do come in!"

The town mouse ducked his head and went inside. Like any country mouse's home, it was nothing more than a little hollow in the ground, with bare walls and a mud floor. But to the town mouse, used to grand houses with wallpapered walls and gleaming floors, it looked very dismal indeed. He didn't want to seem impolite, however, so he simply said, "Why don't we eat outside? It's such a glorious day!"

"Good idea," said the country mouse, and he scampered off to his storeroom to get their lunch. He bustled outside a moment later, carrying an armful of sunflower seeds. "Do help yourself," he said, as he laid them out on the grass.

The town mouse nibbled on a seed. "This is rather plain food," he thought. "Perhaps the next course will be a little more exciting."

The country mouse noticed his cousin wasn't eating very much. "Here," he said, offering him another sunflower seed, "do eat your fill."

"I don't want to fill up on the starter," smiled the town mouse. "I was saving my appetite for the main course."

"Main course?" said the country mouse in surprise. "But this is all there is."

The town mouse was astounded. "This is IT?" he squeaked. "But what do you live on the rest of the time?"

"More seeds," said the country mouse. "Occasionally, there's a strawberry or two, when they're in season..." He tailed off when he saw his cousin's horrified expression.

"No pies?" asked the town mouse. "No sandwiches or muffins or pieces of cheese?"

The country mouse shook his head.

"No chocolate cake or jam tart or ice cream?"

"I've never even tasted them," replied the country mouse.

"My dear cousin," said the town mouse, "you haven't *lived* until you've tasted ice cream." He stood up and pulled the country mouse to his feet. "We have to leave right away," he said firmly. "You're coming to my house for dinner."

"But I've never been beyond the edge of the field before," the country mouse gasped as they scurried to the station.

"Then it's high time you did," answered the town mouse. They hopped onto the train and scrambled onto a window seat. As the train chugged through the countryside, the country mouse stared excitedly out of the window, his nose pressed right up against the glass. The fields gave way to houses and streets, buses and cars, and before long they found themselves in the busy town.

When they stepped outside the station, the country mouse's mouth dropped open. He quaked with terror at the cars that zoomed past, and trembled as an enormous bus screeched to a halt beside them. But the town mouse hardly seemed to notice. "Come on," he said, and dived into the traffic.

By the time they reached the house where the town mouse lived, his country cousin had almost been stepped on, very nearly run over and was utterly exhausted.

"Welcome to my humble home," said the town mouse, and the two mice slipped under the front door.

The country mouse gasped. There were gleaming tiles as far as he could see, walls covered in strange and beautiful flowers, and a crystal chandelier that shone like the sun.

"Are you hungry?" asked the town mouse.

"Ravenous," said the country mouse.

"Then what are we waiting for?" laughed his cousin. The pair ran across the tiles into the dining room and shinned up the leg of the enormous dining table.

"Dinner is served," said the town mouse grandly.

The country mouse's mouth dropped open in amazement. He'd never seen so much wonderful food in all his life. There were mountains of cheese and rows of crumbling biscuits, great bunches of purple grapes and stacks of mouthwatering sandwiches, and, at the far end of the table, more cakes and delicious desserts than he'd ever dreamed of.

"Help yourself," said the town mouse, his cheeks already bulging with cheese.

The country mouse wandered around the table in a daze, plucking a grape here and nibbling on a sandwich there. He climbed all over the cheeses, tasting a mouthful of each different kind.

"Wheee!" his cousin shrieked from across the table, and he slid down a spoon into a bowl of whipped cream.

"Wait for me!" the country mouse shouted gleefully and he ran to join in the fun.

By the time he had stuffed his mouth full of chocolate cake, licked all the frosting off a cherry slice and munched his way stickily through a large strawberry tart, the country mouse decided he felt entirely at home in the town. He was just wiping his paws on a crisp, white napkin when the town mouse called, "Come with me.

I've got a surprise for you." Taking his cousin by the paw, he led him over to a cold glass bowl with huge pink and white balls in it. "This..." said the town mouse dramatically, "is ice cream."

They swung themselves up on a spoon and jumped into the bowl. "It's freezing cold!" exclaimed the country mouse.

"Of course it is," said the town mouse. "Try it."

His cousin dipped a paw into the ice cream and licked it. It sent sweet, icy shivers of delight down the little mouse's spine. "It's heaven!" he sighed, closing his eyes in bliss.

Suddenly, the dining room door flew open and a man walked into the room. Quick as a flash, the town mouse jumped down and hid behind the ice cream bowl. But the country mouse was glued to the spot with fright. "Hide!" whispered the town mouse. "Quickly, before he sees you."

Coming to his senses, the country mouse dived between two scoops of ice cream. It was colder than the middle of winter, but he didn't dare move. He crouched down, shivering, until he heard the sound of the door closing again and saw his cousin's face looking down at him.

"Is-s it s-s-afe t-to c-c-ome out now?" said the country mouse, his teeth chattering with cold.

"Of course," said the town mouse, pulling his cousin out of the bowl and brushing the frost off his whiskers. "Come and eat some apple pie," he said reassuringly. "That will warm you up."

They were just heading for the steaming apple pie at the end of the table when there was a loud "MEOW".

"Uh-oh," said the town mouse.

Before the country mouse could even ask what the matter was, a gigantic, ferocious-looking orange cat leapt up onto the table right in front of them.

"Run for your life!" shrilled the town mouse.

This time, his cousin didn't have to be told twice. The pair fled helter-skelter down the table, with the cat hot on their tails. They shot past the chocolate cake, slipped between two plates and raced around the cheeseboard. Hissing ferociously, the cat bounded after them, knocking glasses over and sending bowls flying in every direction.

The mice reached the edge of the table just in time.

As the country mouse leapt off the table, he felt the cat's claws swish past his back. He landed on the soft carpet, his heart pounding in panic. Behind him, the cat spat with fury as it skidded to the edge of the table, clawing at the tablecloth to try to keep its balance.

"Over here!" squeaked the town mouse, pointing towards a little hole in the skirting board, and the two mice raced across the carpet.

There was a yowl and an almighty crash as the cat fell to the floor, pulling the tablecloth and all the plates and glasses down after it.

Without stopping to look back, the two little mice dived into the hole and collapsed in a heap behind the wall, their sides heaving. "That's just a little drawback of living the high life," panted the town mouse.

"A *little* drawback?" gasped his cousin. "You can keep your high life. I'm off back to the country as soon as I've caught my breath."

"What?" said the town mouse. "And live without all this heavenly food?"

"Yes," said the country mouse firmly. "I'd rather have my peace and quiet than risk life and limb for a pawful of ice cream."

The honest woodcutter

A woodcutter was hard at work chopping down a big tree when his axe slipped out of his hand. It fell with a splash into the nearby river and was carried away by the rushing water.

"Oh no!" the woodcutter cried. He dropped to his knees and thrust his hand into the river, but the torrent nearly swept him away. His axe was long gone. "I only had one axe," he wailed. "Now I have nothing to chop with. If I can't chop wood, I can't earn any money. How will I feed my family?" He felt so hopeless that he sat down, buried his face in his hands and began to cry.

After a few minutes, he heard a gentle voice say, "Excuse me." He looked up to see the god Hermes standing in front of him. The poor woodcutter had never met a god before, and he gazed at Hermes in absolute astonishment.

"Why are you crying?" asked Hermes kindly.

"I dropped my axe into the river by accident," explained the woodcutter sadly. "Without it, I can't chop wood. If I can't chop wood, I can't earn any money to buy food, and my children will starve."

"Perhaps I can help," said Hermes and, as quick as a flash, he dived into the river. A moment later, he popped up a little way downstream. In his hand was a large and extremely beautiful golden axe. "Is this yours?" Hermes called to the woodcutter.

"No," said the woodcutter. "Mine wasn't nearly as lovely as that."

Hermes disappeared under the water again and brought up a beautifully engraved silver axe. "Is this the one?" he asked.

The woodcutter shook his head. "That's not mine either," he said. "Mine was just made of iron and wood."

Hermes disappeared once more. This time he came up with the woodcutter's axe in his hand. "That's the one!" cried the woodcutter, jumping for joy.

Hermes climbed out of the river and gave him back his axe.

"Thank you," beamed the woodcutter. "It may not be made of gold or silver, but to me it's worth more than all the riches in the world."

Hermes smiled. "In reward for your honesty," he said, "you may keep the gold and the silver axes as well as your own."

The woodcutter couldn't believe his luck. "Thank you a million times over," he gasped, and ran to tell his family what had happened.

On the way home, he bumped into another woodcutter. Bursting with excitement, he told the man all about his good fortune. After they had said goodbye, the second woodcutter thought to himself, "Perhaps I can go and get a gold and a silver axe for nothing too." He marched down to the riverbank to try his luck.

There was no sign of Hermes or anyone else, so the woodcutter threw his axe into the middle of the river and waited for the god to appear. Nobody came.

"Maybe he'll come if I cry," thought the woodcutter, and so he began to bawl as loudly as he could. To his great satisfaction, Hermes appeared before him. The woodcutter peeked out at the god between his fingers.

"Whatever's the matter?" Hermes asked kindly.

"I've dropped my axe in the river," blubbered the woodcutter. "Please could you help me get it out?"

"Of course," said Hermes, and he dived into the water.

The woodcutter rubbed his hands in glee. "Rich!" he muttered. "I'm going to be rich!"

A moment later, Hermes appeared a little way downstream, holding a beautiful golden axe. "Is this the one?" he called.

"Yes," cried the woodcutter. "That's mine."

Hermes waded over to the bank and climbed out. "Are you sure?" he asked, bringing the axe closer so that the woodcutter could see it more clearly.

The woodcutter's eyes gleamed at the sight of the precious gold. "Yes, yes," he said eagerly. "It's definitely mine." He reached out to grab the axe.

Hermes took a step back and frowned. "You fool!" he said. "For being so greedy, you have not only lost your own axe, but this one too." With that, Hermes tossed the axe carelessly over his shoulder and walked away into the trees.

The woodcutter's face fell as he watched the golden axe flash through the air, splash into the river and get swallowed up by the foaming water. He never, ever saw it again.

The stork who outfoxed a fox

In the woods by a lake, there lived a sly fox. He was well known for playing practical jokes, and he was rather proud of his reputation too. But because the animals in the woods knew the fox so well, none of them fell for his tricks any more. Whenever he invited them for dinner or told them anything unusual, the animals would just laugh and say to one other, "Pay no attention. He's just trying to fool us."

One afternoon, the fox saw a stork land by the edge of the lake. "We have a newcomer," he remarked to some squirrels who were scurrying around in the branches overhead. "I think I'll go and welcome her to the area."

"Don't think you can trick a stork," warned the squirrels. "Storks are very clever birds. They wouldn't fall for your tricks."

"Oh, don't you think so?" said the fox. "Well, just watch this." He sauntered out of the trees and strolled up to the stork.

"Good afternoon to you," he said politely.

"Good afternoon," replied the stork, peering down her long beak at the fox.

"I haven't seen you before," said the fox casually. "Are you new around here?"

"Yes," replied the stork. "In fact, I've flown a very long way. I'm just stopping here for a few days' rest."

"Oh really?" said the fox. "Well, allow me to be the first to welcome you." He cocked his head to one side and smiled a wide, crafty smile. "In these woods," he continued, "we usually share our food with newcomers. Could I invite you to dinner?"

The stork looked delighted. "Thank you," she said. "That's very kind."

"I'll just go and get some food ready then," said the fox. "Why don't you come over in about an hour?"

"Very well," nodded the stork.

"You'll find my door beneath the big oak tree," said the fox, and he trotted off into the woods.

When the stork arrived for dinner, the fox was as pleasant as ever. "Welcome," he said, and brought out a big, shallow dish of steaming vegetable soup. The stork's stomach rumbled hungrily.

"It's our custom to eat from the same dish," said the fox as he set the dish down on the table. "Is that all right with you?"

"Of course," said the stork.

"Splendid," replied the fox. "Do help yourself."

The stork dipped her beak into the soup to try some. But because the dish was so shallow and her beak was so long, she could only scoop up the tiniest drop.

The fox, meanwhile, settled down opposite her, and began to lap up the soup with his tongue. The stork watched forlornly as he lapped and lapped.

"My, it is delicious," murmured the fox, "even if I do say so myself." He glanced at the stork out of the corner of his eye. "Aren't you hungry?" he smirked, and lapped up some more.

The stork tried to eat some more soup. She dipped the tip of her beak in again, but she couldn't scoop any up. Then she tried putting her whole beak in sideways, but it didn't fit. The more soup the fox lapped up, the lower the level dropped and the more impossible it became for the stork to eat any at all. She watched miserably as the fox licked the dish clean.

When the fox had finished the last little drop, he sat back and patted his full belly. He looked at the stork's long face and grinned. "Did you enjoy that soup?" he asked.

The stork took one look at the fox's smug face and realized that she'd been tricked. But she pretended not to have noticed. "It was lovely," she said graciously. "Thank you so much."

"The pleasure was all mine," answered the fox, trying to keep a straight face.

Later on that night, as the stork waded around in the lake trying to catch some fish to fill her empty belly, she racked her brains for a way to pay the fox back. When at last she caught a glistening fish in her long, thin beak, she suddenly had an idea.

In the morning, she went to see the fox. "I'd like to invite you for lunch to repay your kindness," she said.

"Really?" said the fox, looking surprised.

"Yes," said the stork. "Come to the lake at one o'clock. I'll have everything ready." And she stalked off into the trees.

A burst of giggles came from a branch overhead. "Watch out," called a squirrel. "That bird is going to get you back."

The fox shook his head. "No chance of that," he said. "You can't outfox a fox!"

That afternoon, the fox arrived at the lake, ready for his lunch. "Let's use your custom of eating our soup from the same dish," said the stork, and she brought out a tall jar with a long, thin neck. "Don't be shy," she urged the fox. "Do start."

The fox looked at the jar uncertainly. He stood up on his

back legs and rested his paws on the top. A delicious smell wafted up from the soup and made his mouth water. He stretched his neck and just managed to dip the very tip of his tongue into the soup.

The stork leaned over and slipped her long, thin beak down into the jar. "Delicious," she said, swallowing a large beakful of soup, "even if I do say so myself." She smiled at the fox, who was staring forlornly at the neck of the jar. "Not hungry?" asked the stork innocently.

The fox tried again to dip his tongue into the soup, but he couldn't reach at all now that the stork had eaten some. He licked a couple of drops that had spilled over the side, but that only made him hungrier than ever. He sat down and watched unhappily as the stork finished off every last drop.

Gales of laughter came from a nearby tree. "Serves you right!" scolded the squirrels, who had been watching with glee. "That stork's gone and beaten you at your own game!"

How bees got their stings

"Buzz off!" shouted the queen bee angrily as a big hairy hand broke into her hive. But the hand simply brushed the furious queen and her worker bees aside and scooped out all of their precious, golden honey. The bees buzzed and buzzed in protest, but there was nothing they could do to stop it. You see, in those days, bees were just harmless, fuzzy insects with no way at all of defending themselves.

"We can't go on like this," said the queen bee in despair. "Every time we nearly have a hive full of honey, someone breaks in and steals it all."

The worker bees murmured their agreement.

"Enough is enough," said the queen bee firmly. "Come along, all of you. We're going to see the great god Zeus."

They flew off at once, in the biggest, buzziest swarm anyone had ever seen. They blotted out the sun as they flew overhead, and people stopped to look up in wonder as they passed.

The bees flew up through the fluffy white clouds and high into the sky above. They flew right past the north wind and over a rainbow, and at last they came to Zeus' palace.

"What's all this?" said Zeus when he saw the enormous swarm.

The queen bee bustled up to the god and hovered in the air in front of his nose. "Good afternoon, Zeus," she said, dancing a curtsey. "I have come to see you about a most important matter."

The great god bowed politely to the tiny queen. "In that case," he said, "please come inside and explain."

"Very well," said the queen bee, and she flew in through the open door with her entire swarm following behind.

"Do sit down," Zeus said to them. The bees settled all over the polished marble floor, looking for all the world like a large, fuzzy rug. "Your highness," Zeus said to the queen bee, and he laid a red velvet cushion on a throne for her to sit on.

"Thank you," said the queen bee. She settled on the cushion, delicately folded her wings and cleared her throat. "All summer long," she began, "my workers slave away, gathering pollen from countless flowers and making it into honey. But people simply break into our hives whenever they feel like it and steal all of our honey. We have no way of defending ourselves against them." The queen quivered with emotion as she spoke. "I'm appealing to you, as one ruler to another, to help us."

Zeus was as fond of honey as anyone, but he didn't like to see the queen bee so upset. So he racked his brains to think of a solution. Eventually, he came up with an idea. "I think I can give you a way of defending yourselves," he said. "But it would be a shame if nobody could ever eat honey again. So if I give you a weapon that will make people respect you more, will you promise to use it sparingly, and to allow them to take a little honey now and then?"

"Of course," said the queen bee, and her subjects nodded enthusiastically.

"Very well," said Zeus. "Go back to your hives and I'll let

you know when the weapon is ready."

After the bees had left, Zeus went to his workshop and began to design a weapon so tiny that it could be fitted to the tail of a bee. It was very delicate work and took him several days. When he had finally finished, he sent a message to the queen bee. She returned, bringing all of her many subjects with her, and Zeus fitted each and every bee with the miniature weapon.

"This weapon," Zeus explained, "causes a painful sting. It will work as many times as you want it to, but I want you to promise that you'll only use it when it's absolutely necessary."

"We promise," chorused all the little bees. They flew away, wiggling their tails with pleasure, as pleased as punch with their new weapons.

All afternoon, they hummed as they worked, gathering nectar and making it into a fresh batch of honey.

The very next morning, just as the queen bee was eating her breakfast, a fat, groping hand pushed its way into the hive and broke off a piece of honeycomb right in front of her nose.

"Sting the hand!" shouted the queen bee, and three worker bees dived at the hand and stung it as hard as they could.

"OUCH!" came a yell, and the owner of the hand wrenched it back out of the hive.

"It worked!" exclaimed the queen, and a buzz of excitement went around the hive.

The next day, another hand reached in and tried to scoop out some honey. This time, ten bees zoomed over, their tails ready and quivering. "What are you waiting for?" cried the queen bee. "Sting the hand! Sting the hand!" So all ten bees dived gleefully onto the hand and stung it for all they were worth. Its owner yowled in agony and hauled his hand out of the hive as quickly as he could.

After that, there was no stopping the bees. Giddy with their new power, they stung people for stealing their honey; they stung people for touching their hive; and before long, they even began to sting people for just *looking* at their hive.

Zeus knew nothing of this until one day he asked one of his servants to go and collect some honey to spread on his bread. The servant turned pale at the mention of honey, but he didn't dare disobey his master. "Right away," he gulped, and hurried off to the hive.

Half an hour later, the servant burst back into the palace. He was in a terrible state. He had red sting marks all over his arms and legs, and on his face too. He flung himself on his knees in front of Zeus and burst into floods of tears.

"What on earth happened to you?" Zeus exclaimed.

"I tried to get you some honey for your bread," wailed the servant. "Honestly I did. But I didn't even get to the hive before all the bees came and stung me to bits."

"What?" roared Zeus. "I gave them those weapons to protect themselves, not to sting people senseless!"

He stormed straight to the queen bee's hive. As he approached it, all the bees swarmed out to greet him. But when they saw his thunderous expression, they hurried back inside the hive in alarm.

"Come back here this instant!" bellowed Zeus.

The bees peeked out fearfully. The queen bee flew outside, looking more than a little sheepish.

"You ought to be ashamed of yourselves," raged Zeus, "for being so mean with your honey and so generous with your stings. From now on," he continued, "you may each sting once, and once only. When you do, you will not only lose your ability to sting, but your life as well."

The bees took his words to heart and, from that day to this, they have been more generous with their honey, and a *lot* more careful with their stings.

The little mouse
and the ferocious lion

"I really must gather some seeds to store for the winter," thought the little mouse as she scurried along, "and I must remind the children to wash behind their ears." She was so deep in thought that she wasn't paying much attention to where she was going. She came to a steep hill and began to climb it.

The grass on the hill was golden and the ground felt unusually warm beneath her feet. "What a strange hill this is," she said to herself. Stopping for a moment to catch her breath, she noticed something very strange. The whole hillside was moving gently up and down beneath her. "Goodness me," she thought. "It's almost as if it's breathing. But whoever heard of a hill that could breathe?" She poked the ground with her paw to see what it was made from.

Suddenly, the whole hill shuddered violently. The little mouse lost her balance and tumbled head over heels, landing with a bump on the cool, green grass at the bottom of the hill. She watched with eyes as round as saucers as the strange, golden hill rose up and up before her.

All of a sudden, she realized that it wasn't a hill at all. It was an enormous lion. "Eeek!" squeaked the little mouse in terror. She turned tail and fled for her life. But with an ear-splitting roar, the lion slammed his paw down on her tail, pinning her firmly to the spot.

"How DARE you wake me up," the lion growled ferociously.

"I'm r-really s-s-sorry," stuttered the mouse, her whiskers trembling in terror. "I thought you were a hill."

"A hill?" the lion snarled, curling his lip to show two rows of large, glistening teeth. "Well, this hill is hungry. It's time for a bite to eat." He opened his large, terrible jaws.

"Stop!" shrieked the mouse. "Please stop! If you let me go, I'll repay you. I promise."

The lion paused and looked down at the tiny creature. "YOU?" he said in disbelief. "What use could a little thing like you be to ME?"

"You never know," said the mouse in a very small voice. "If you ever got into trouble, I might be able to help you out."

The lion threw back his head and roared with laughter. He laughed and laughed until tears streamed down his face. "I've never heard anything more ridiculous in all my life," he gasped, holding his sides.

"It's not that funny," said the mouse, folding her arms indignantly. But this just made the lion laugh even more.

"It's hardly worth eating a little morsel like you anyway," he sighed, when he'd finally managed to control himself. "Seeing as you've put me in such a good mood, I'll let you go." He took his paw off the mouse's tail.

"Thank you," beamed the mouse. "You won't regret it."

"Get out of here," chuckled the lion, "before I change my mind." So the mouse scurried home, as quickly as her legs would carry her.

A few days later, the little mouse was scampering through the forest when a furious roar broke the silence and sent birds fluttering in all directions.

"That sounds just like the lion," she thought. A moment later, there was another, less powerful roar, followed by a low, rumbling groan. "It sounds like he's in trouble," the little mouse said to herself, and she hurried off in the direction of the noise.

She reached a clearing and there was the lion. He was in a very sorry state indeed. He was caught in a hunter's net and was wrestling with it desperately. But the more he tried to break free of the net, the more entangled he became.

"Hello, lion," said the little mouse.

The lion stopped struggling and gave a huge, miserable sigh. "I expect you've come to gloat, now that I'm powerless," he said.

"Not at all," said the little mouse. "I've come to pay you back for setting me free – just like I promised."

The lion rolled his eyes. "Not that again," he growled. "I'm having enough trouble myself, and I'm much bigger and stronger than you." And he went back to wrestling with the net.

"Stop thrashing around for a minute," said the little mouse briskly. Then she clambered onto the lion's back and began to gnaw through the ropes, one by one. After just a few minutes, she hopped back down onto the ground. "There you go," she said.

The lion stood up and the net fell to the ground. He was free. "Amazing!" he said, shaking his magnificent mane. "Whoever would have thought that a little pipsqueak like you could save a lion's life? Thank you, my little friend. Thank you from the bottom of my heart."

The flying tortoise

"I might go for a little fly about after lunch," one tortoise said to another.

"Fly?" coughed the other tortoise, choking on a leaf. "What are you talking about? Tortoises can't fly!"

"Do you know of any who have tried?" asked the tortoise.

"No..." replied his friend.

"Well then," said the tortoise. "How do you know we can't? We might be really good at it."

His friend blinked at him slowly. "I really don't think it's a good idea," she said.

But the tortoise wasn't listening. He was staring dreamily up at the sky, picturing himself swooping about like a swallow. "Soaring over the treetops," he murmured. "Looping the loop. Ah, yes. I'm sure there's nothing quite like it."

He munched thoughtfully through the rest of a dandelion leaf, and then heaved himself onto his feet. "I can't wait any longer," he said. "I'm going to do it now." And he headed off into the open field, with his friend following behind.

The tortoise began by stretching out his wrinkly legs, one by one, to warm up. "I'll jog in that direction," he said, pointing along a path through the long grass. "And then, when I'm running at about fifty miles an hour, I'll take off."

"Right," said his friend doubtfully.

The tortoise took a deep breath and then started off down the path, going very, very slowly. He was just getting into his stride when a fieldmouse scampered across the path.

"Watch out!" panted the tortoise. "You're on the runway."

The mouse stopped and looked back at him in surprise. "Runway?" it said. "What runway?"

"I'm about to take off," explained the tortoise.

"But tortoises can't fly," the mouse giggled.

"Watch this," said the tortoise, and he tried to launch himself into the air. He lifted his front feet off the ground, pushed with his back legs... and landed on his nose in a patch of prickly thistles.

"That was a short flight," tittered the mouse.

"You see?" called his friend. "Tortoises can't fly – we're just not made for it. Give up and come home."

"All I need is a bit of height," protested the tortoise, as he disentangled himself from the thistles. "Tortoises aren't very good at taking off, it seems. But once they're in the air, there's no stopping them."

"I wouldn't be so sure," said the mouse, shaking its head. "Tortoises don't have any wings. You need wings to be able to fly – like a bird."

"Of course!" exclaimed the tortoise. "Why didn't I think of that? I'll ask a bird for some help."

His friend let out a groan. "Why don't you listen to us?" she said. "Tortoises can't fly."

But the tortoise wasn't paying attention. He was too busy peering up at the sky, looking out for birds. After a couple of minutes, an eagle came into sight. It was soaring high in the air, the sun glinting off its golden feathers.

"Hello up there!" yelled the tortoise, as loudly as he could.

The eagle, whose hearing was as sharp as his eyesight, began to descend, spiralling gracefully down. It landed in front of them and folded back its wings. "Can I help you?" it asked.

The tortoise was lost for words. He'd never seen an eagle up close before. He gazed, open-mouthed, at the glorious golden bird until his friend nudged him. "Ah – yes," he stammered. "Erm – I could do with some help flying. That is, if you'd be so kind. I'd be all right if I could get into the air, but I'm having a little trouble taking off."

88

The eagle tilted its head to one side and stared at the tortoise through piercing amber eyes. "I didn't think tortoises could fly," it said.

"They *don't* fly, generally," explained the tortoise, "but that's only because they can't get off the ground."

"Perhaps there's a reason for that," said the eagle.

"Oh, but won't you help?" pleaded the tortoise. "All you'd need to do is carry me up into the air. Then, when we've reached a good height, you can let me go. I'll take it from there."

The eagle gave him a shrewd look. "Very well," it said. "I'll help."

"I really don't think this is a good idea," muttered the tortoise's friend.

Beating its huge wings, the eagle lifted a little way off the ground and took hold of the tortoise's shell with its talons. "Ready?" it asked.

"Ready!" replied the tortoise enthusiastically. His stomach lurched as they took off, but he watched with giddy excitement as the ground dropped away beneath them.

"Are you all right?" called the eagle.

"F-fine," said the tortoise, somewhat shakily.

The eagle climbed higher and higher until all the tortoise could see of his friend was a little dot in the field below. Any minute now, the eagle would let go and he'd be flying like a bird. The thought suddenly made him feel slightly ill.

"Are you sure you want to do this?" asked the eagle.

"It's now or never," gulped the tortoise. "Whenever you're ready," he croaked, trying his best to sound brave.

The eagle glanced down at the field below. Positioning himself carefully, he let go of the tortoise's shell.

The tortoise plummeted toward the ground at great speed. He gasped as the air rushed past him, and then began to flap all four of his legs. He flapped and flapped for all he was worth, but it didn't seem to have any effect.

"It's all in the technique," he thought determinedly. He stretched out his neck and tried to loop the loop, but this only made matters worse. He began to tumble helplessly head over heels. As the ground whooshed up at him, the tortoise's life flashed before his eyes. He thought longingly of slow strolls through the woods and lazy lunches that lasted all afternoon. "I'm too young to die!" he wailed, and tucked his head inside his shell.

Down on the ground, a small crowd had gathered to see the tortoise fly. They all stared, aghast, as he hurtled down from the sky and dropped like a stone into a haystack.

High in the air, the eagle wheeled around a few times, looking down into the hay. Then it gave a satisfied nod and flew off.

"I tried to stop him," sobbed the tortoise's friend, "but he wouldn't listen." There was a long, stunned silence. Then, all of a sudden, the tortoise's head popped out of the top of the haystack.

"You're alive!" squeaked the mice.

"It's a miracle!" cried the tortoise's friend.

The tortoise clambered dizzily out of the hay. "You were right, you know," he said. "Tortoises can't fly. And anyway," he added with a wrinkly grin, "they much prefer to walk."

The slender reed and the olive tree

Down on the riverbank, a slender reed was dancing in the breeze. The slightest breath of wind sent her swaying this way and that. Her movements were so graceful that even a dragonfly paused to watch, hanging motionless in the air before darting downstream in a blur of shining sapphire.

The sturdy olive tree standing on the other side of the river wasn't so impressed. "What a weedy reed you are," she mocked. "Why do you let yourself get pushed around so much? You fall over at even the hint of a breeze. What would you do if a real gust of wind came? You'd never last!"

But the reed didn't answer. She just curtseyed sweetly to the next passing breeze, and danced on merrily into the afternoon.

The days slipped by, and soon, after the flowers had folded away their petals ready for winter, a strong wind began to blow. It swept in from the north, sending clouds scudding quickly across the sky. Storming into the field where the olive tree stood, it buffeted her trunk and rustled her branches.

"Stand firm, little reed!" called the olive tree. "Stand firm like me or you'll be swept away." And the olive tree braced herself stiffly against the fierce wind.

The reed said nothing. She met the wind with a courteous bow, and let it sweep her around, bending her this way and that. She danced more beautifully than she'd ever danced before.

The wind grew stronger and stronger. It swooped down and flung itself violently against the olive tree's branches, but the stubborn tree refused to bend. "I'll never give in to you!" she shouted defiantly. But just at that moment there was a terrible CRACK, as one of her branches snapped in half.

"How dare you!" gasped the tree, trembling with helpless rage. But the wind just sped away across the field, tossing the branch aside like a broken toy.

As the storm died down, the olive tree suddenly remembered the little reed. "If the wind was able to break my strong branch," she muttered to herself, peering across the river, "that weedy reed must be long gone." But, to her great astonishment, the reed was still there. And, what's more, she was hardly even out of breath. By bending to the wind, the little reed had ridden the storm without a care, and had come out the other side still dancing.

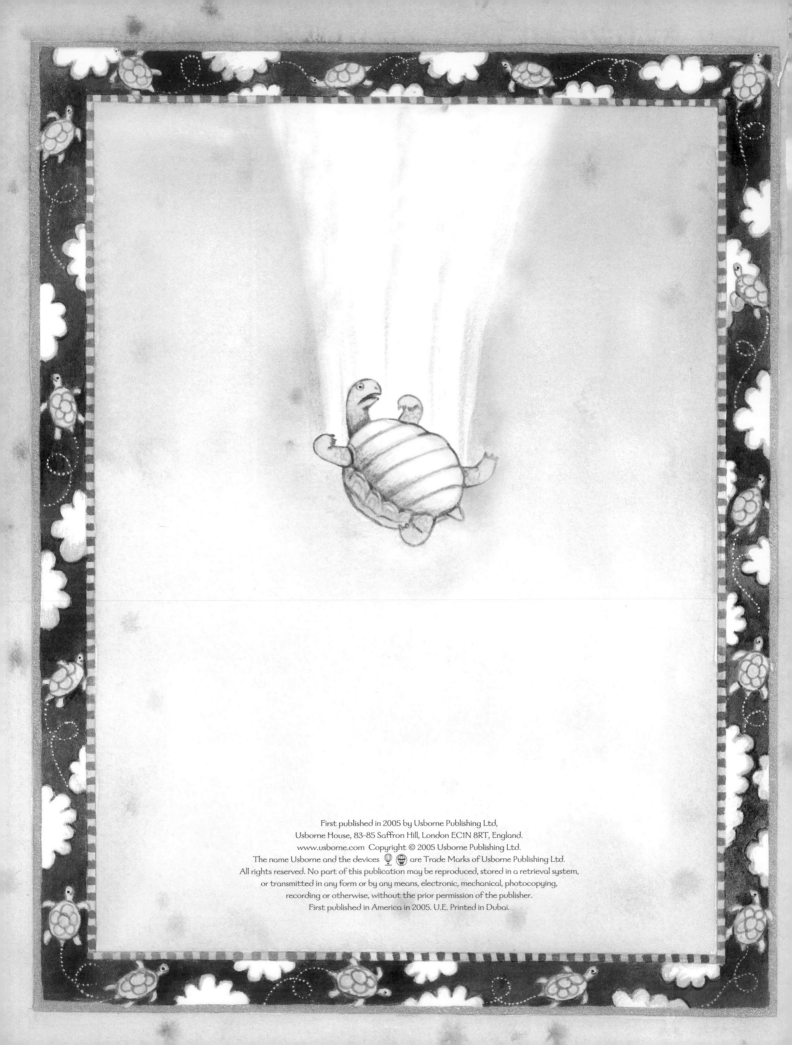